Christmas Stories

MERRIGOLD PRESS • NEW YORK

The Singing Christmas Tree

A little deer came skipping through the snowy woods. His eyes were shining, and his heart felt as light as a snowflake from all the wonderful things he had seen in town. The little deer could not wait to tell his mother about the bright lights, so he hurried through the woods to find her.

"Oh, Mother!" cried the little deer when he finally saw his mother.

"I went to town and peeped in the window of a house. There was a tree inside, glittering and shining, with stars in its branches— red and green ones, blue and white ones, too. And it was hung with bright balls that sparkled the light all over the room!"

The mother deer nodded slowly. Her eyes shone, too.

"That was a Christmas tree," she said. "At Christmas, people deck their trees with lights and toys and shining things."

"Christmas tree!" whispered the little deer. "Oh, Mother, I want a Christmas tree, too, with lights!"

Oh, how the mother deer wanted a tree for her baby! She thought and thought and thought, and at last an idea came to her.

"Follow me," she said.

The mother deer took her baby farther into the woods and showed him a small tree in a clearing. "We'll put berries on the branches," she said. "We'll put tasty shoots on them, and tender roots."

But when the tree was dressed, it was not bright and shining like the tree in town.

"Never mind," said the mother deer. "Wait until morning. Then we will come to look at it again."

The next morning, the mother and baby deer went deep into the woods. Close to the clearing they stopped and peeped in. The little deer was amazed. Icicles hung from his Christmas tree, shining with sunrise. Snowflakes sparkled on it, in red and green and blue and white. And on all the branches were bright singing birds, eating the berries and shoots.

"Merry Christmas!" they sang on that early Christmas morning. "Merry Christmas!" they chattered between bites.

The little deer nuzzled his nose in his mother's neck. "It's a beautiful tree!" he whispered. "Much more beautiful that the tree in town!"

The mother deer smiled happily. And one by one, the other animals came to look at the little deer's wonderful singing Christmas tree. They all agreed it was the best tree ever.

The Christmas Sled

It is Christmas morning. Dana and David run downstairs to see what Santa has left for them. David finds a tricycle. He is happy. But even happier is Dana when she sees what Santa has left for her. "A sled!" she says. "Oh, it's just what I wanted."

Dana looks at her new sled. She likes the bright red wood.
David looks at Dana's new sled. He likes the silvery runners.
After breakfast Dana says, "I want to go outside and try my new
sled." Everyone else decides to go outside, too. They get all bundled up.

Dana climbs to the very top of the hill and gets on the sled.
"Here I come," she calls out. She whizzes down the hill. "I want to
do that again!" she says. And she does—two more times.

Then Dana lets David take a turn on the sled. "Wheeee," he
says as the sled flies down the hill.

After a few more rides, the family starts back home. They stop to watch the skaters on the pond and make a snowman. When they are back in their warm house, David and Dana each have a big dish of ice cream! "Mmmmmm," they say.

At bedtime, Dana says to Father, "Do you know what? I love my new sled. It's the best Christmas present I ever got!"

Mr. Hedgehog's Christmas Present

London was even more wonderful than Mr. Hedgehog had
imagined. The stores were a miracle of Christmas lights and finery.
Even the mice went about with presents for their friends.

"I should like to get a present for Mrs. Hedgehog!" said Mr.
Hedgehog to himself.

What should it be?

Not a fur coat. Mrs. Hedgehog had a fine one of her own.

Not a diamond tiara. That would be too heavy for her head.

Surely not a bottle of scent. Hedgehogs like the smell of fern and hawthorn.

Suddenly something lovely caught Mr. Hedgehog's eye. A bright red apple lay in the clean snow, lost and forgotten.

Mr. Hedgehog picked it up and brushed off the snow. He polished it with his mittens. Solemnly he offered it to his wife, saying, "A merry Christmas, my dear!"

Mrs. Hedgehog kissed him. "Thank you," she said. "I'll make us a big, sweet, warm apple dumpling."

The little Hedgehogs one and all, smacked their lips and shouted, "Merry Christmas!" again and again.

Arm in arm, the Hedgehog family hurried home to their cozy burrow, which soon smelled of apple and spice and crisp pastry browning — the very merriest kind of Christmas smell!

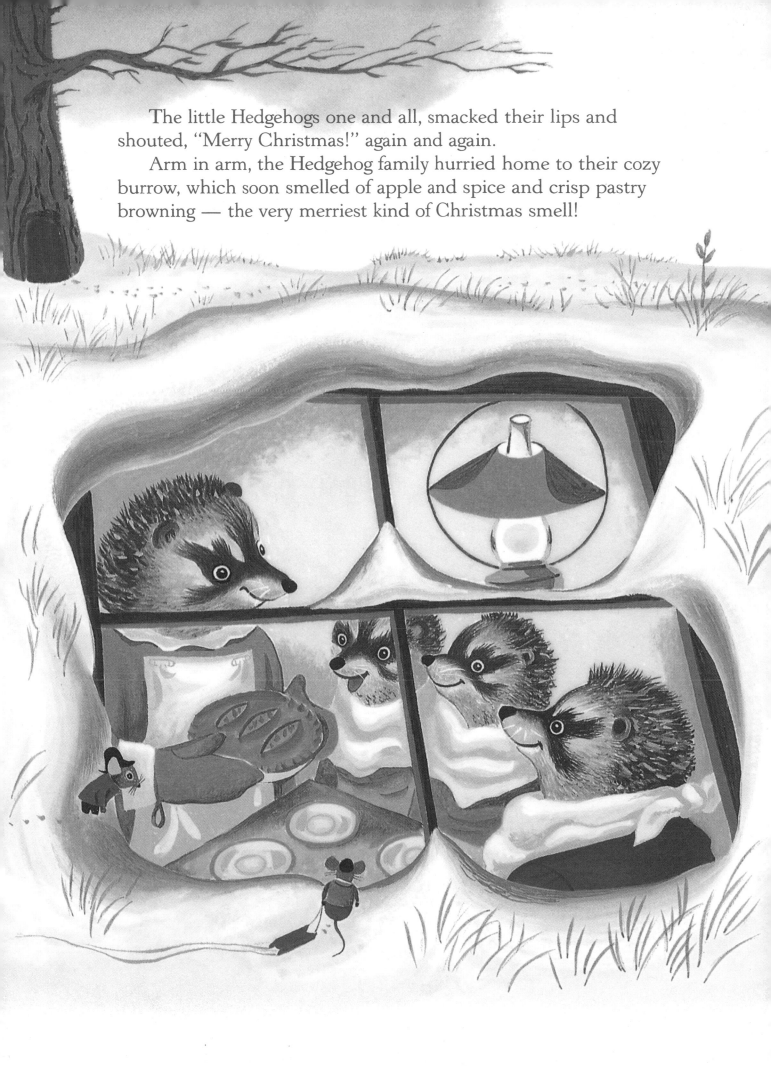

Here Comes Santa Claus

It is Christmas Eve. Sarah and Katie are fast asleep. But Mitzi the kitten is not asleep. She hears the sound of bells jingling in the distance.

Here comes Santa Claus! Mitzi can see his sleigh and reindeer flying through the starry sky.

"Whoa, Dasher. Whoa, Prancer," says Santa. The reindeer will land on the rooftop so Santa can climb down the chimney with his big sack of toys.

Mitzi runs downstairs and sees Santa putting lots of toys and presents under the Christmas tree. There's even a tricycle for Sarah and a big stuffed panda for Katie. Santa winks at Mitzi.

"I have a present for you, too," he says. Mitzi purrs. Santa has to go now. His work is done. Mitzi watches the reindeer pull Santa's sleigh up, up into the sky.

Christmas morning is here at last. Hurry, everyone. Mitzi wants to show Sarah and Katie what Santa has brought.

What wonderful presents!

"Look, Mommy," says Sarah, "Santa has brought Mitzi a present, too!"

Merry Christmas, Mitzi.

Merry Christmas to everyone.

The Christmas Tree

It was nearly Christmas—time to get a Christmas tree. Father Bear and the Baby Bears went into town to buy a tree. Father Bear and the Baby Bears looked all around the Christmas tree lot.

In the middle of the lot stood a beautiful tree. "I think that one will do just fine," said Father Bear. Father Bear tied the tree to the top of the car, and the Baby Bears helped.

When they got home, Father Bear sawed off the bottom of the tree so it would fit in the tree stand. Mama Bear watered the tree to keep it moist. Grandma Bear helped the Baby Bears make stars and paper chains. Grandpa Bear and Sister Bear put lights on the tree.

Sister Bear put her star on the very top of the tree.

Father Bear served hot chocolate, and they all sat down to look at the tree. Everyone felt tired and happy.

In the morning, the Baby Bears ran downstairs and found the tricycles Santa had left for them under the beautiful tree. They were pleased indeed!

A Very Small Christmas

I wonder if the chipmunks know,
When everything is white with snow
And night starts coming very fast,
That Christmas time is here at last?

And do the little chipmunks go
To sleep, quite early, in a row—
With Christmas dreams inside their heads
And extra blankets on their beds?

And do they hop up just at dawn
And put their robes and slippers on
And hurry out to peep and see
If someone brought a Christmas tree?

If someone did, I wonder who?
Their chimney's small to wriggle through!
Their Christmas tree must be a twig—
But maybe chipmunks think it's big.

I hope it's trimmed with sunflower seeds,
And peanuts, too, and icy beads,
And lighted candles (birthday size)
To make a grand chipmunk surprise!

Authors and Illustrators

THE SINGING CHRISTMAS TREE
By Kathryn B. Jackson
Illustrated by Richard Scarry

THE CHRISTMAS SLED
By Carol North
Illustrated by Terri Super

MR. HEDGEHOG'S CHRISTMAS PRESENT
By Kathryn B. Jackson
Illustrated by Richard Scarry

HERE COMES SANTA CLAUS
By M. Hover
Illustrated by Christopher Santoro

THE CHRISTMAS TREE
By Carol North
Illustrated by Diane Dawson

A VERY SMALL CHRISTMAS
By Kathryn B. Jackson
Illustrated by Richard Scarry